Starway Station

Written by
Jane Clarke

Illustrated by
Dynamo

It was the Solar System summer holidays. Spaceships of every kind were stopping at Starway Station to take a break on their journeys from planet to planet.

Zap and Astra were helping their mum in the café. They watched from a porthole as a rocket car drew up and threw open its doors. A five-tailed squonk from Mars jumped out and rushed through the airlock, closely followed by its Martian owner.

Zap quickly pressed the translator button on his watch as the squonk scurried up to him, wagging its tails.

"Is it tame?" he asked the squonk's owner.

The Martian nodded his head and wobbled his tentacles. "She's only a baby; she won't hurt you," he told Zap.

"Welcome to Starway Station!" Zap stood on tiptoe to tickle the squonk behind its rubbery pink ear. Pleased little squonking noises came from its trunk.

"Here, squonky," the Martian called, as he headed for the café. His pet scurried after him.

"Baby squonks are cute," Astra giggled, "but they can turn nasty when they're fully grown. I'd like to have a pet dog. They only have one tail, but they're loving and loyal, and lots of fun. I wish Mum would let us have a pet."

"So do I," Zap sighed. "I'd like a cat – they make *puurfect* pets … "

"Pets?" Mum emerged from the kitchen with a tray of freshly made stardust spacewraps.

"As I've told you before, pets are a lot of work," she said. "We don't have time to look after them. We have our hands full with running the café and keeping up with repairs. Robo rats took another chunk out of the bathpod wall last night."

"They nibbled at the wall of our bedpod, too," Zap told her.

"But we spotted the hole and mended it with the moonbeam welder before anything got sucked into outer space," Astra added hurriedly.

"Phew!" Mum sighed with relief.

There was a loud "*squonk*" from behind the café counter. Mum hurried to serve the customers.

"I'm so sorry to keep you waiting," Mum apologised to the Martian. "What would you like to eat?"

"Everything!" said the Martian, waving his tentacles.

"*Squonk!*" agreed the squonk.

"I have to make more spacewraps," Mum told Zap and Astra, after she'd finished serving the Martian and the squonk. "So I need you to check the rest of the Station for robo rat holes."

"I'll get the welder," said Astra.

*****

"There's another hole here!" Zap shone the magnifier on the bath pod wall.

Astra directed the moonbeam welder at it. "That makes sixteen today!" she groaned. "Robo rats are real pests."

"Nearly done," Zap told her. "We just need to check the transporter toilet."

The sign above the keypad by the toilet door said "occupied". Zap and Astra waited and waited and waited …

"Someone's transported themselves in, and forgotten they have to flush to transport out again," Zap said. "That's the third time this week!"

Astra knocked on the door. "Are you all right in there?" she asked. From behind the door, something made a strange noise that sounded like a cross between a meow and a bark.

Zap and Astra looked at one another. The noise didn't translate. "There's an animal in there!" Zap exclaimed.

He tapped the emergency number into the keypad and the toilet door swished open.

"*Meowoof!*" said a furry little creature with pointed ears and a striped tail. Around its neck was a note. It said: *Please look after this tabrador.*

"*Meowoof!*" the tabrador said again, putting its head on one side.

"It must be a cross between a labrador dog and a tabby cat!" said Astra, as she stroked the tabrador's fluffy brown and yellow head.

"I think she's a girl." Zap pointed to her fluffy collar.

The tabrador wagged her tail and purred.

"Awww!" Zap murmured. "She'd make a perfect pet. Maybe Mum will let us keep her."

"Let's find out!" Astra scooped up the tabrador and the twins raced to the kitchen.

"We found Tabbie in the transporter toilet," Zap told Mum. "She needs a home. She's been abandoned!"

"Can we keep her? *Pleee-ase*," Astra begged.

Tabbie squeaked, "*Yippeek!*"

"She's a cute little thing," Mum smiled. "But pets need a lot of looking after, and we just don't have the time."

"*We'll* look after her," Zap declared.

"We will," Astra agreed, "and we can train her."

"In that case," said Mum, "she can stay for a day or two and we'll see how you get on."

****

"Sit!" Astra commanded for the tenth time, and for the tenth time, Tabbie rolled over and purred.

"Fetch!" Zap threw a ball. Tabbie ran off with it.

"Stay!" he commanded, but Tabbie just wagged her tail and trotted off.

"Tabradors are very hard to train," Astra sighed.

"Astra! Zap!" Mum called. "Come and see this!"

Zap and Astra raced into the kitchen, followed by Tabbie.

Mum pointed to the bottom of the wall around the air vent. It was covered in scratches.

Zap and Astra looked at Tabbie. Her ears drooped.

"Tabrador claw marks!" Mum sighed. "It's bad enough having to deal with robo rat damage every day, without tabrador destruction, too. Tabbie will have to go. We'll find her a new home."

"But she's only been here a few hours … " Zap began.

There was a loud scratching noise behind the air vent. Tabbie pricked up her ears. Her whiskers whiffled.

"*Meowoof!*" Tabbie scrabbled at the vent.

Astra knelt down and peered into the air vent. "Robo rats!" she exclaimed, pulling the grill away from the wall. "Tabbie's found a nest!"

Tabbie dived into the hole, meowoofing loudly.

Three huge robo rats shot out.

"*Meowoof!*" Tabbie chased them across the floor of the cafe and into the airlock.

Zap, Astra and Mum grinned as the robo rats scurried out the other side and jumped onto the roof of a Saturn Saucer that was about to take off.

"Saturn is where robo rats come from," Astra commented, as the saucer disappeared into outer space.

"I hope they stay there!" Zap exclaimed.

Tabbie looked up at them. "*Yippeek!*" she yipped.

Zap and Astra looked pleadingly at Mum.

"Of course Tabbie can stay!" Mum laughed. "She'll chase away any robo rats that turn up at Starway Station."

"Yay!" Astra jumped for joy.

Tabbie purred and purred, wagging her tail so hard it was a blur.

"A tabrador's the best pet in the whole Solar System!" Zap laughed.